How to Get Your TEACHER Ready for School

by Jean Reagan
illustrated by Lee Wildish

Hodder
Children's
Books

For teachers everywhere. You are truly amazing.

–J.R.

First published in the United States by Alfred A. Knopf, an imprint of
Random House Children's Books, a division of Random House Inc., New York.

First published in the UK in 2018 by Hodder Children's Books.

Hodder Children's Books
An imprint of Hachette Children's Group
Part of Hodder & Stoughton
Carmelite House, 50 Victoria Embankment
London, EC4Y 0DZ

A CIP catalogue record of this book is available from the British Library.

ISBN: 978 1 444 93036 8
1 3 5 7 9 10 8 6 4 2

An Hachette UK Company
www.hachette.co.uk
www.hachettechildrens.co.uk

You're ready for the first day of school.
But what about your teacher?

Make her feel welcome with
an extra big smile. Then . . .

HOW TO WELCOME YOUR TEACHER:

⭐ Sing a "Good morning" song!

⭐ Show her your favourite spots in the room.

If she asks, "Why don't I have a tray?" point to her very own desk.

Whisper, "I know where the bathroom is, if you ever need to go."

BATHROOM →

School days are busy, so make sure she's ready for . . .

⭐ Art – button up
her smock *before*
a disaster.

⭐ Lunch – share your secret:
"You get extra spaghetti
if you *say* please."

⭐ Library time –
show her where
to find the iguana
books.

When it's time to go home, tell your teacher,
"Good job today! Ready for tomorrow?"

As the year gets going, there are lots of special things
to get ready for. Like . . .

CLASS PHOTO

⭐ Remind your teacher, "No messy snacks."

Chocolate cupcakes? Nope!

Sugary doughnut? Nope!

Juicy, juicy strawberries?

Nope!

⭐ Take a look at her
hair. Does she need
a comb?

★ Then, instead of saying, "Cheeeeeeese!" say, "Teeeeeeeeeeeeeeacher!"

Perfect!
Now it's time for . . .

a CONCERT!

If your teacher's feeling nervous, show her how to *tiptoe*, *tiptoe*, *tiptoe* to the side of the curtain. Pull it back a teeny bit. Once she spots her family, she'll be ready to "*La la la!*"

Some days — even when your teacher is ready —
things don't work out as planned:

★ The class pet escapes.

★ All the planets crash
down as the head
teacher pops in.

★ Or rain ruins everything.

How can you help? Quick — hand her a favourite book!

When the day *finally* ends, say, "Don't worry.
Tomorrow we'll *all* be ready for a brand new day."

And on that brand new day, you will make sure
your teacher has the best day . . .

Everyone get ready to:

⭐ Have a dance party.

⭐ Do some gardening.

⭐ Count to 10 with your toes.

⭐ And if you still have time, tell your favourite jokes.

Your teacher knows a lot, but not *everything*!
So ask, "Are you ready to be . . . amazed?"

THEN TEACH HER ALL ABOUT:

⭐ Big, stinky flowers of the jungle.

⭐ What elephants, naked mole rats, hummingbirds, and Venus flytraps like to eat.

⭐ The sounds of a howler monkey.

"GAHOO! GAHOO! GAHOO!"

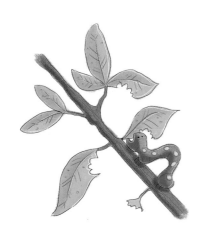  

⭐ How sometimes magic . . . happens . . . very . . . slowly.

When spring comes, it's time for Sports Day!

HOW TO GET YOUR TEACHER READY FOR SPORTS DAY:

⭐ Make sure her whistle works.

Tweet! Tweet!

Tweet! Tweet!

TWEET!

✩ Help pick out her fastest shoes. Double knot the laces.

✩ Does she have her water?
Her hat?
Her sunscreen?

Now everyone shout, "READY, SET . . .

. . . GOOOOOOOO!"

Why not surprise your teacher one day by making the day all about her!

HOW TO CELEBRATE YOUR TEACHER:

⭐ Everyone dress in her favourite colour.

⭐ Say "teacher" in all the languages your class knows.

⭐ Give her something special, but definitely not . . .
- A big, stinky jungle flower.
- An ice sculpture for her desk.
- An already-opened box of chocolates.

As the year ends, get your teacher ready for one last thing . . . *goodbye.*

HOW TO SAY GOODBYE TO YOUR TEACHER:

* Decorate a thank you card with all the things you learned.

* Surround her for a whole class hug.

* Give her one last extra big smile.

Now your teacher's ready for a new class.
You're ready, too, for a whole new year. But . . .

your teacher will remember you forever.
And you'll always remember her.

You are my favourite teacher ever!

I don't have a gift,

but I drew an apple to give to you.

I like it when we play and you teach me new things.

To the best teacher,

Your lessons are the best.

Collect more bestselling *How to* books . . .

For fun activities visit www.hachettechildrens.co.uk